WILD RETURN

WILD HEART MOUNTAIN: WILD RIDERS MC

BOOK FIFTEEN

SADIE KING

WILD RETURN

I'm a soldier looking for a second chance. She's the woman whose heart I broke. My final mission—win back my cupcake.

Four years ago, I faced an impossible choice. I left the mountain, my MC, and Sydney, the woman I loved.

Now I'm back as security for the brewery where she works, and the tension is thick between us.

Someone's siphoning beer in the dead of night, the security cameras aren't working, and every clipped order she barks makes me want to pin her against a fermenter and remind her who we were.

Protecting the brew is the job. Winning back my cupcake? That's a mission I refuse to lose.

Wild Return is a steamy, forced proximity romance between an ex-military biker and the curvy girl he must convince to give him a second chance.

Copyright © 2025 by Sadie King.

All rights reserved.

No part of this book may be reproduced in any form or by any electronic or mechanical means, including information storage and retrieval systems, without written permission from the author, except for the use of brief quotations in a book review.

NO AI TRAINING - This book may not be used to train AI.

Cover designed by Cormer Covers.

This is a work of fiction. Any resemblance to actual events, companies, locales or persons living or dead, is entirely coincidental.

This book was written by a human and not by AI.

Please respect the author's hard work and do the right thing.

www.authorsadieking.com

1
SYDNEY

My heeled boots clack on the concrete steps as I descend into the brewery cellar. The sweet smell of hops permeates the air, and light slants through the single high window. I stomp over to the rows of stacked kegs, slicing through dust motes in my wake.

Of all the men to walk into the clubhouse last night, Viking was the last one I expected to see. He's military for life; he made that clear four years ago.

I thought I was over him, but seeing the way he waltzed in as if he'd never left, with every club member slapping his back as if he's a returning hero and not the man who left me in pieces four years ago, enrages me..

The peacefulness of the brewery cellar usually calms me, but not today. My body vibrates with energy as I pull up the inventory app.

I move down the rows of beer, counting kegs and punching numbers into the app, but my mind keeps returning to Viking. The way he slid off his bike as if no years had passed, the new scar on his left temple, the soft way he looked at me, and the old nickname on his lips brought back too many memories. Memories that took four years and five continents to erase. And with one word, *cupcake,* it all came flooding back.

I stop between rows B1 and B2 with no idea how many kegs I've counted.

"Damn," I mutter to myself.

I stomp back to the cellar wall and begin my count of the bottom shelf again. They're stacked two deep, and I count in twos until I reach twenty-four at the end of the row.

I make a note in my app, and my mind thinks about the time Viking picked me twenty-four wild daisies, one for every week we'd been together, and gave them to me tied up with a piece of string.

I dried those damn daisies as if they were red roses and kept them for weeks in a ceramic pot by my bed.

Until he left, and I chucked them in the compost.

The sound of voices pulls me out of my reverie. Barrels's booming voice precedes him down the cellar steps.

He's followed by a dozen hungover resort guests, all wearing matching t-shirts with the face of one member of their party on it. The man in question has disheveled hair and red eyes and looks like he's about to puke into one of our kegs.

We make good money from the brewery tours and

especially the bachelor parties, who spend big in the tasting room.

Barrels gives them the full tour, describing the precise temperatures needed to store different types of beer in detail. I can tell the group doesn't care, that they just want to get to the tasting, but Barrels doesn't notice or he's deliberately drawing it out. He was a first-class sergeant in the army, and with his curt manner and formidable frown, none of the men are going to ask him to get on with it.

I sidestep around the group and duck into the next row of kegs. The tall rows muffle their voices.

I begin my count on Row C1, starting with the top shelf and counting in twos. This is the IPA special that's shipping out on Friday to a new distributor on the East Coast.

The count is soothing and keeps my mind off Viking.

As I get to the bottom row, Barrels moves the tour group out of the cellar, and it descends into peace once more.

"Two, four, six..." I stop abruptly and peer between the kegs. There's an empty space in the back row. The kegs are stacked beside each other in pairs, and there's a spare space where one keg is missing its partner.

I walk slowly down the row, peering in between the kegs to check if there are any other empty spaces.

There's only one missing, and I would put it down to a staking error except it's the second time it's happened this month. Once is an error; twice is suspicious.

I tag it as missing in the inventory, and it flags as a red mark in the app.

I glance up at the busted security camera in the corner of the cellar. Even if it were working, the angle might not see into this corner. I've been meaning to get it fixed for the past few weeks, but there's always something else to do.

I sigh and move it up my mental to-do list.

Without warning, my mind cuts to last night and Viking's throaty laugh as he stood around the fire pit with Raiden and Hops and Barrels.

I shake my head, trying to clear the memory, and stuff the tablet into its case and head upstairs.

The office is open plan, and my desk is to the right, looking out of the glass window to the brewery floor. I nod to Isla, who sits at the desk next to mine on the days she comes in. She looks like she's about to say something but must think better of it when she sees my expression.

I slide the tablet onto my desk, but the missing keg is playing on my mind.

Barrels must have finished the tour by now, and I decide to find him.

His office is at the other end of the metal walkway that overlooks the brewing tanks. The brewery floor is the heart of the brewery, and giant metal vats line one wall, each brewing up a different type of beer.

Before I get to the stairs that lead down to the brewery floor, the door to Barrels's office opens, and he steps through.

"You got a minute?" I ask.

He frowns. "If you're quick. I've got to help Charlie in the tasting room."

It's likely he doesn't want to leave his wife alone for long if there's a group of men in there. So, I get straight to the point.

"There's another keg missing."

He looks up sharply and stops. "Which one?"

"From the IPA line. The order going out on Friday."

"Shit." He runs a hand through his short hair. "That's two in one month."

I press my lips together, not liking what I have to say next. A lot of the staff working here are from the club, and if I voice my suspicions, it throws suspicion on everyone.

"I think someone's taking them."

I expect Barrels to be upset, but he nods once. "Perfect timing. I just hired extra muscle."

Viking steps through the office behind Barrels. His large frame and height mean he's as wide as the walkway. His eyes lock on mine, and a corner of his mouth tilts.

My stomach drops. "You're hiring him?"

Barrels holds his hands up. "I don't have time for this. Whatever is in your past, you two need to sort it out. I'm needed in the tasting room. Sydney, show Viking around and take him through the security protocols." He lowers his voice. "And fill him in on what you just told me."

Barrels heads down the staircase to the brewery floor and disappears into the tasting room, and I'm left facing

Viking. He towers over me, and I refuse to strain my neck to look up at him.

"I'll show you the cellar."

To get to the cellar, I need to get down the metal stairs on the other side of Viking. I glare at him pointedly, but he doesn't move.

"The cellar is down the stairs."

I stare at him, wondering when he's going to take the hint and move out of the way. He doesn't.

"The stairs are behind you."

Viking smirks. "I know."

Instead of going down the stairs first like a polite human, he shifts his body sideways and offers a hand, indicating for me to go first.

I squeeze past him so close to the railing it imprints on my back, but I still brush against him as I go past. There's a moment of pressure when his hard body is against mine. His scent of leather and coffee beans encases me for a moment, making my head spin and my heart race. A hundred memories of his body pressed against mine flit into my brain.

"After you, cupcake," he murmurs. And his voice is an echo from the past, scraping every raw part of me.

My head spins, my heart races, and there's a tug in my core.

Then I'm past him and gripping onto the railing to keep my balance.

I inhale sharply and suck in long breaths as I descend the stairs. I don't dare look back at Viking. I don't want him to see the effect he's having on me.

I've got to keep this professional, find the keg thief, and whatever I do, don't melt for the man who broke my heart in two.

2

VIKING

*A*s I follow Sydney down the stairs to the brewery floor, my gaze travels down the back of her neck and the thick rope of dark hair that swings between her shoulder blades.

It's longer than I remember, hanging a good few inches past her shoulders.

Her knee-high boots leave a sliver of thigh where they don't quite meet her skirt and make her go slow on the stairs. I'm right behind her, and her thick plait is too tempting. I have to know if her hair still has the same silky texture and if she still uses citrus-scented shampoo. I reach my hand out and capture her plait in my fist.

She goes dead still as I run my hand down the length of her plait from her scalp to her shoulders. The locks are silky smooth, a balm against my callused palm.

"What are you doing?"

She keeps looking ahead, and I tug on the end of her plait before letting it drop.

"Did you just pull my hair?"

Her tone is annoyed and incredulous and brings back memories of the two of us sparking off each other. Sydney was always challenging. That's why I loved her so much. Why I still do.

"I did."

I wait for her to spin around, to see the fire in her eyes and the retort that's sure to follow. But she doesn't even glance back.

"Touch me again and I'll report you for harassment."

Not the playful retort I was expecting.

She marches down the stairs, and I follow her. It was never going to be easy coming back, but I didn't expect her icy response.

We get to the cellar, and Sydney spins around.

"You know what? You can show yourself around. The cellar's down there. There's a missing keg in row C1. You're security. You figure it out."

Her eyes flash dangerously, and it's a relief to see her fire. Better than her ignoring me.

"And next time you want to touch my hair, ask me first. The answer will always be no."

She stomps off, and I watch her go. Her hips sway in the fitted skirt she's wearing, and her boots clack angrily across the floor.

It's later that evening, and the brewing shift has left for the day. Barrels rushed out half an hour ago. He's in an awful hurry to get home these days and to his family.

The last time I was back between deployments, the Wild Riders were single men. Now they're coupled up, and there are kids and babies crawling around the clubhouse.

Time moves on, and I hope like hell I haven't missed my chance at that.

Barrels told me Sydney would take me through the lock-up procedure, but I haven't seen her since this morning and I dare not go into the office.

Yesterday she threw a drink at me, and today she stomped off in a huff. I deserve it, I guess. But I sure as hell would like her forgiveness.

I hear the clip of Sydney's boots coming down the metal stairs before I see her. I lean on the door frame that leads to the tasting room to watch her descend the stairs.

She's filled out in the four years since I last saw her. Her curves are more pronounced, more womanly. There's a new confidence about her. Sydney was always confident, but now she's downright bold.

She avoids looking at me as she marches past and into the tasting room. "Barrels insisted I show you how we lock up."

I follow her into the tasting room.

Lights buzz overhead, illuminating the rows of wooden bar stools and tables. Sydney strides between them to the double doors of the main entrance. She pulls on the doors, checking they're locked.

"Charlie shuts everything down at the end of the day, but I always give it a check."

She speaks in a clipped and professional tone. She's

got her armor up, and I didn't help matters by pulling her hair earlier like some kid in the schoolyard.

I stride to the double doors and pull on them, making them shake.

Sydney folds her arms over her chest and glares at me. "You just saw me check them."

I scan the edges of the door, looking for signs of forced entry and weak points. With two kegs missing in the past month, it's got to be theft, which is why I'll be spending my nights on site for the foreseeable future.

"Just doing my job."

She huffs out a breath and strides toward the door that leads back to the brewery floor. I'm halfway across the room when she flicks out the lights. The sudden darkness disorients me, and my foot catches on a bar stool. There's the scrape of metal against floor as my knee connects with the stool.

"Fuck."

I hear a pleased huff from Sydney and smile despite the throb in my knee. She wants to forgive me, but I'll have to endure pain and humiliation first. Fair enough, for what I did to her.

I follow the thin streak of light to the brewery floor and find Sydney waiting with a smirk on her face.

"How long you gonna keep punishing me for, cupcake?"

Her smirk turns to a frown, and she turns away. "As long as it takes."

The door between the tasting room and the brewery

floor is made of thick metal. Sydney heaves it shut and slams the bolt home.

"The tasting room entrance is for the public. Once it's shut for the day, this can be locked up."

I fall into step beside her as she strides across the brewery room floor and to a silver panel linked to the tanks.

"This is the fermenter gauge. In the high season we have a night shift running, but at other times, Barrels has a remote link. But I like to give it a check before I leave."

"Barrels said you like to work late."

She peers at the fermenter gauge and punches in a number. "Did he now?"

She's not giving anything away. I want to ask why she works so hard. If it's because she doesn't have anyone to go home to. But I steer the conversation to something safer.

"I hear you got back into town six months ago."

She raises her eyebrows. "You seem to know a lot about me."

I've kept track of Sydney's every move for the last four years, but if I tell her that now, she's likely to accuse me of stalking her. "And that you moved in with your brother. How is Nate?"

The fermenter gauge beeps, and she turns a dial one notch to the left.

"He's just gotten married again. Hang around long enough and you'll meet his new wife."

She snaps the lid shut and strides to the next tank.

I press my lips together and ignore the dig.

"Have you worked at the brewery since you got back?"

"I thought you knew everything about me?"

I lean against the wall and watch her pressing buttons and adjusting like a pro. It doesn't surprise me that six months in and she's practically running the place. Sydney is smart and competent, and Barrels obviously trusts her. She's the operations manager, and when he told me that, I swelled with pride. Sydney's come a long way in four years. And she won't admit it, but she might not have done if she had been saddled with me.

With the gauges checked, we head down to the cellar.

The cool air makes my arms prickle, and I resist the urge to fold them around Sydney. We walk between lines of kegs as Sydney flicks out lights and checks packing notes. When we reach row C1, there's a printed piece of paper stuck to the end of the row.

Small-Batch IPA - MISSING 1

Sydney pauses to glance at the sign, and I'm reminded why I'm here.

I stroll to the door that leads through the loading bay and check that it's secure. When I turn around, Sydney's waiting for me at the bottom of the steps.

"I usually lock the cellar door, but if you're patrolling here, I guess you want it open."

"Correct."

I follow her up the stairs, my eyes drawn to her swaying plait. Four inches longer. Marking the time I wasted without her.

"Sydney…" I begin, not sure how to go on but needing to get through to her. "About yesterday…and before that."

She spins around, and her eyes blaze in the dim light. "No." She shakes her head. "We're not doing this. There's no need to drag up the past."

"But I want to explain. You're obviously still mad at me."

She reaches the top of the stairs and grasps the heavy door in her hand.

"You did explain. And I get your reasons."

I join her at the top of the stairs, and she slams the door closed. It shuts with a loud clang that reverberates through the building.

"We're done here."

She spins around and heads up the metal stairs to the offices. I jog to catch up to her, and we don't say anything as we reach the office.

Hers is the only desk with the computer screen still on. While she shuts it down, I gather her purse from the floor and her jacket from the back of her chair. She looks at me, confused.

"What are you doing?"

"It's dark. I'm giving you a lift home."

She glares at me, then shakes her head softly. Her expression goes from anger to pity.

"I'm not that young girl anymore, Viking. I learned to take care of myself."

"You always could take care of yourself, cupcake," I reply softly.

Her eyes blaze. "Don't call me that. You have no right to call me that."

She snatches her jacket out of my hand and swipes her purse off me. She marches to the exit, and I lean on the edge of her desk as I watch her go. She heads into the night, and the door swings shut behind her.

I sit on the edge of her desk for so long that the office sensor lights turn off and plunge me into darkness.

I walked away from Sydney once; I'll never do it again. However long it takes, I'll convince her that I'm back for good.

3
SYDNEY

*T*he aroma of fried garlic hits me as soon as I open the door to Nate's place. I shrug off my coat and hang it on a hook in the corridor. The sounds of kids' laughter comes from the kitchen, and I push open the door.

Dora holds a wooden spoon in the air as she marches around the kitchen island with Maisie trailing behind.

Nate is at the stovetop sauteing onions, and Freya has her arms wrapped around his waist. Nate turns from the stove, and Freya steps back. His arms shoot around her, like they can't bear not to be touching each other.

"Auntie Syd!" Maisie breaks from formation and races toward me. She barrels into my legs, and I scoop her up into a hug.

"You want to be in our marching band?"

Her wide eyes stare at me hopefully, and usually I love messing around with my nieces, but tonight all I want to do is get to the sanctuary of my room.

"Another time."

I set her down, and Maisie frowns at me. Dora marches past and bops her on the butt with the wooden spoon. Maisie spins around, her frown focused on her sister.

"Hey," says Nate, "we've got to stir the dinner with that spoon. No butts."

The girls break into peals of laughter, and Dora holds the spoon in the air, declaring it the Butt Spoon.

They race off into the living room, leaving Freya and Nate laughing.

I've been living with my brother since I came back to Wild Heart Mountain. He's never made me feel like I don't belong here, but with his two girls and a new wife, I've been thinking about my next move. I can't live with him forever.

"You joining us for dinner tonight?" Nate asks.

Most nights we eat all together, but I don't feel like company tonight.

"I'm not hungry," I lie. "I'll grab a snack later."

Nate narrows his eyes at me. Damn sibling perception. He can tell I'm not myself, and he must guess why.

Nate was deployed when Viking left me, so he didn't see the worst of it. When my brother came back on leave, he was the one who encouraged me to still go traveling without Viking. But he says nothing.

"You want a glass of wine?" Freya grabs a bottle from the fridge and tops up her and Nate's glasses.

"No thanks. It's been a long day. I'm going to head upstairs."

If I drink tonight, I might get sentimental, and that's the last thing I want.

I grab a water glass and fill it from the high-tech water filter Nate has installed on the faucet. While I wait for my glass to fill, I watch Nate and Freya together.

He sets down his glass of wine and slides his hand around her waist. They shuffle-dance to the pop music blaring from the speaker, which I'm guessing is Dora's choice. Freya leans her head on his shoulder and closes her eyes.

It must feel nice to have someone solid, someone you can rely on, someone to come home to after a shitty day.

I grab my water and head upstairs. That kind of easy love just isn't for me.

Once Freya and Nate got together, I moved into the turret suite where Freya was staying when she was the nanny, before she became the wife.

I slide my purse off my shoulder and dump it by the two-seater, then set my glass on the coffee table. I unzip my knee-high boots and slide my feet out of them. The carpet is soft under my feet, and I wiggle my toes.

My neck is stiff, so I rub the back of it, trying to ease the tension. Damn Viking for coming back and disturbing my equilibrium. It took me four years to find peace after he ditched me. It took that long to stop missing him every day, and more importantly to learn to love myself again.

Now he's back, wanting to talk about the past and disturb my hard-won peace.

In the corner of my room is my large backpack. For four years it held all my possessions in the world as I backpacked around the globe until I stopped in Australia to work.

What was supposed to be a six-week gig working in a bar ended up with me running the place for two years. It was only when the owner offered to sell it to me that I realized I wanted to come home. I missed the mountains. So I packed up my belongings and set off for a final adventure, arriving on Wild Heart Mountain just before Christmas.

I crouch beside my backpack and lift up a worn strap. There's dirt woven into the fibers, and the fabric is threadbare near the zipper. I tug it open and reach into a side pocket and pull out a bundle of letters held together with twine. They're blue airmail paper, and the scrawl across the front is barely legible. My name with Nate's address. I refused to give Viking a forwarding address, but Nate forwarded on all his letters whenever I stopped long enough to have an address.

I finger the string that ties them together. It's been a long time since I looked at his letters. My fingertips hover over the top one.

No. Not tonight. I chuck the letters back into the backpack. I've wasted enough time thinking about Viking today. I will not let him invade my peace any more than he has already.

I take a seat at my craft table and click on the desk lamp.

A half-finished figurine awaits on my painting station. She's a warrior with a wild red braid and gleaming armor. I select a fine-tipped paintbrush and a teal color for the outline of her shield.

As my brush moves, my breathing steadies. But thoughts of Viking invade my mind. The way he pulled my hair like we were kids, the tingle I felt down my spine when his fingers brushed against my back, the way my skin prickled when he called me cupcake.

I squint at the figurine, focusing harder as I switch colors and apply the paint to another highlight.

After an hour of crafting, my mind is clear, and my head aches from concentrating so hard.

I set the warrior down to dry.

Tomorrow I'll ignore the letters, ignore *him*, and get on with work and the inventory audit. I've crafted my own peace, and I won't let a man disrupt it.

4

VIKING

*I*t's just before three when I push open the glass door to the communal office, holding a steaming mug of coffee.

Sydney's in the meeting with Barrels and the rest of the team for their daily check-in. I know because I hacked her work calendar, so I'd know when she wasn't at her desk.

I leave the steaming mug on her desk and slip out of the office door.

I've set up a security hub in the room next door. It's taken me a week to install new security cameras and a bank of monitors. I checked back on all the security footage we have, but it's patchy and there was no trace of our keg thief.

It's kept me busy, and I've given Sydney her space. But now it's time to win her over.

A glass wall separates our offices, and I take a seat in front of my wall of monitors just as the door to the meeting room opens. I resist the urge to smile to myself at the perfect timing. The coffee will still be warm at her desk.

Davis gave me shit over at the bar when I ordered a double with oat milk and half a shot of vanilla. When I explained it was for Sydney, he gave me a knowing look and informed me she takes it with a full shot of vanilla now. He mumbled something about all the women turning the bar into a gourmet coffee place and how he has to keep three different kinds of milk stocked.

I keep my gaze on the monitors, but my whole body is focused on Sydney. She reaches her desk and takes a seat. In my peripheral vision, I see her freeze when she notices the coffee.

I imagine her brow pulled together in a frown as she half gets out of her seat to look around.

"Who put this here?" I hear her say through the glass wall.

It's only Isla and Charlie in the office, and they both just came out of the meeting.

Sydney's gaze rests on me, and I keep my expression neutral and my eyes on the screens. I'm glad there's a glass wall between us, or she'd notice how tense I am.

She huffs and then sits down. I wait for her to drink the coffee, but it stays stubbornly on her desk.

I get up from my post, and without glancing her way, head along the walkway to do my rounds.

When I come back an hour later, Sydney is nowhere to be seen. I walk past her desk, and the coffee is sitting in its mug, untouched. At least she didn't throw it at me, so that's a small victory.

The next day I do the same thing. Sydney's stubborn, but I'm persistent.

This time when I get the coffee from Davis, I also beg a cookie from Maggie. She's just baked a batch of chocolate chip for the afternoon crowd, and I snag one and put it on a plate for Sydney. She works so hard I never see her eat, and from what I've observed, she skips lunch more often than not.

When she comes out of her daily meeting, the coffee and cookie are waiting on her desk. I keep my eyes on the screens, but I feel her gaze sweep over me.

She sits down again, and I get up to do my rounds. When I stroll past the office an hour later, there are lipstick marks on the mug and half the cookie is missing.

I hum to myself as I head to the security room.

My phone buzzes as I sit down, and I answer to a number I don't recognize.

"Chris. It's Paulie."

In the club I'm known as Viking, and it stuck as a nickname in the military. The use of my given name has me sitting up straight.

I worked with Paulie for a few years until he left the military. Last I heard, he was running a security firm, hiring out private contractors for work in the Middle East.

"I'm in need of a reliable man for contract work."

Paulie cuts straight to the point. "It's a six month contract. Good money. All expenses paid."

My gaze darts to Sydney. She stares at her computer and twiddles a pen between her fingers. I promised I wouldn't leave again. And I meant it.

"Sorry, Paulie. I've got something going on back on the mountain."

"The pay's good." Paulie continues as if I haven't just turned him down. "You work a couple of contracts for me, and you'll have your mortgage paid off."

Something stirs inside me. That kind of money could give me security. It could set me up for life. I'd never worry again about where money was coming from.

Sydney stirs at her desk, and my gaze locks on her. She keeps her gaze on the computer screen as she lifts up the coffee mug and takes a sip.

A smile creeps across my face.

"Sorry, Paulie. The answer's still no."

Paulie chuckles. "I'll text you what I'm offering, then you tell me if it's still a no. I'll leave it open for a week."

The next day as I'm pushing open the door to the office with Sydney's coffee balanced in one hand and a chicken sandwich in the other, the door to the meeting room bursts open. They must have finished early.

I place the plate and mug on Sydney's desk, and when I turn around, she's right behind me. It's the closest we've been since she showed me around last week, and I suck in a sharp breath as I catch the scent of her perfume, Coco Mademoiselle. I'd pick that scent out anywhere.

Her gaze locks on mine, and she murmurs, "Thanks."

The spatter of rain on the skylights makes us both look up. When I glance down again, she's sitting down at her desk with her back to me.

"There's a storm coming in. I'd better go check for leaks."

She doesn't respond, and I make my retreat. But an hour later, the coffee cup is empty.

I come in early on Thursday to help secure tarps over our outdoor silos. They're predicting gale-force winds by the weekend, and most of the guys are out helping secure the place.

Raiden leads a team up the mountain to check in on the locals and see if anyone needs help to prep for the storm.

I duck away at three to get Sydney's coffee, but I'm needed with a jam in the loading bay, so I don't have time to see her drink it.

I'm securing the bolt on the sliding door when my phone buzzes. It's a text from Paulie.

I'll add an extra 15%

.   .   .

Two days ago, he sent through an eye-watering number that he's offering me for six months' work. I hover over the text, thinking how one six-month stint could set me and Sydney up for the future. But there will be no future if I leave her again. Even if we were at the stage of talking, let alone talking about a future together, one hint that I'm leaving will have her shields going up, and I'll lose any ground I've made.

But how do I know there will ever be anything with Sydney?

I ignore the text from Paulie and instead type a text for Sydney, asking her to meet me to talk. My finger hovers over the send button.

Sydney made it clear that she doesn't want to talk, and if I force the issue before she's ready, I risk losing the progress I've made this week.

I delete the message without sending it and slide my phone back into my pocket.

Friday arrives with winds so strong my motorbike sways on the mountain roads, and I dig my thighs in to keep her under control. Any sensible guy would take a car, but the bike is all I own.

It's raining when I leave the clubhouse for the short walk over to the brewery. I hold my leather jacket over the coffee mug, taking it slow so as not to spill any. Rain soaks my skin in minutes, and wind whips at my hair. But I don't spill a drop.

Sydney is out of her meeting early, and she frowns at me when I hand her the coffee.

"You're soaked."

I shrug. "But your coffee's warm."

I hand it directly to her, and her gaze meets mine over the mug.

"Thank you." She takes a sip, keeping her eyes locked on mine.

Her eyes sparkle deep emerald, and there's a warmth in them that I haven't seen since I came back. She looks beautiful, and for the first time since I came back, I believe I may have a chance.

"Sydney I…"

The office door slams open, and Barrels charges in. "Will that loading bay door hold in the winds?"

Sydney turns away and sits at her desk. The moment's gone, and I walk out with Barrels, answering his questions about the coming storm.

5

SYDNEY

Saturday afternoons are my favorite time at the brewery. In the quiet season, when we're not brewing seven days a week, I'm usually the only one here.

I let myself in and go to disarm the alarm but stop when I realize it's already disabled. Someone else is here.

With Freya and Nate all loved up at home, I was hoping to get some quiet time at the brewery and get ahead on work for next week.

We postponed yesterday's shipment because of the high winds on the mountain. It wasn't safe conditions for a truck to drive on these mountain roads. It means juggling the schedule and rebooking with our customers, and I'd rather get that done today so I can start fresh next week.

Nate didn't want me to go out in the storm, but my SUV is an all-wheel drive and it can handle a bit of wind and rain. Besides, we're only under a severe thunder-storm watch.

Rain beats down on the skylights and rattles the windows. The wildness of the storm soothes my turbulent mind, reminding me there are forces out there greater than myself.

I'm focused on a spreadsheet showing inventory and those missing two kegs, so I don't hear Viking enter the office until he's right by my desk.

"What are you doing here?"

I jump at the sound of a human voice and spin around to find Viking. His arms are folded over his chest, and he's got a frown on his face.

"You scared me."

"You shouldn't be out in this weather."

He sounds just like my brother. The only difference is that Viking has no right to look out for me.

"I'm fine. The worst of it is supposed to hit overnight."

Viking glances out the window where the thunderous clouds make it seem more like night than late afternoon. I was so engrossed in my inventory that I didn't notice how dark it had gotten.

"Go home, Sydney, before it gets too dangerous to drive."

I clench my teeth in irritation. Viking has no right to tell me what to do. He gave up the right to protect me four years ago when he chose the military over me.

"I'm just fine here."

He shakes his head. "This storm is going to be bad. You need to leave while you can."

I raise an eyebrow. "Like you left."

Viking huffs in irritation. "This is no time to be stubborn, Syd. You need to leave."

He's right, but damned if I'm going to let him know that. I've got good tires, and I don't live far away. I just need another hour to figure this out.

"I don't leave."

He shakes his head. "Please don't be stubborn about this. I'm just trying to keep you safe."

"I've learned to look after myself. And I'll keep myself safe. Thank you."

I'm being childish, but I can't help it. I don't want him to think he can tell me what to do.

Viking saunters out of the room, and I smile.

A gust of wind rattles the skylights and shatters my moment of victory.

He's right. I should get home, but I'm going to stay here as long as I can just to piss him off. It's going to take more than a few cups of coffee to get back into my good books.

Twenty minutes later, Viking's back. I feel his presence before I hear him.

"They've closed the roads at the top of the ridge." Viking's tone is low but firm.

I keep my focus on the spreadsheet in front of me. It's

a twenty-minute drive home, and the worst roads are further up the mountain.

"I'll make it through the worst of it."

He sets a soggy cardboard box on my desk, and from inside the box he extracts two silver mugs and a brown paper bag.

"At least have something to eat while you're here."

He puts one of the mugs on my desk. Steam leaks from the vent in the top of the mug, and the aroma of milky coffee wafts out with it. My gut clenches at his thoughtfulness. After four years, he remembers exactly how I like my coffee.

"Thank you."

"I caught Davis as he was locking up. They've closed the restaurant for the afternoon, and he's heading home."

He looks at me pointedly. "Maggie was already gone, but I made us some sandwiches and snagged a couple of cookies from the kitchen."

He pulls a chocolate chip cookie out of the bag and hands it to me wrapped in a napkin. Viking makes it hard to stay cross with him.

As I reach for the cookie, there's a boom of thunder straight overhead. My body jolts, and my hand bumps up against his. Viking wraps his fingers around my wrist, and my pulse thumps against his fingers.

"I got you, Syd," he whispers.

My gaze meets his, and memories flood in from a time before. A time when I believed we'd have each other forever.

I wrench my hand away, and it's trembling. I tell myself it's from the thunder and not from his touch.

"I'm fine."

Viking steps back, putting distance between us. The rain on the roof turns more violent, and the building shakes with a gust of wind.

"What are you doing here anyway?" I ask.

"I wanted to make sure the place was secure for the storm."

He looks away, and there's something he's not telling me.

"Didn't you do that yesterday?"

He nods and I raise my eyebrows, waiting for him to go on. "What is it?"

He sighs. "The two lost kegs both went missing on a weekend."

"You think someone's breaking in here on a Saturday?"

"Maybe. I found some weak points in the cellars." He averts his gaze and takes a bite of his sandwich.

"You're doing a stakeout?"

He shrugs. "I was going to monitor the cameras from home. It's unlikely anyone would be out in this storm. But now that you're here, I'm not leaving until you do."

"Oh." I chew my sandwich. It's not just me who will have a treacherous drive home but Viking too. And he's on a motorbike.

"Can't you work from home with your laptop?" he asks.

He looks so desperate I almost agree to leave. But I

want to prove the point that I'm my own woman and I look after myself, and I don't need a man to take care of me. I'll give him a lift home when I leave so he doesn't have to go on his bike. But I'm not going to tell him that yet. I'll do a final check downstairs, then I'll get out of here.

I push my chair back. "I need to go down to the cellars and count out the kegs from the latest brew."

My words are cut off by the howl of the wind, and something thumps against the roof. We both glance up as the fluorescent lights flicker then die.

The office is plunged into darkness as there's another thump from outside.

"What was that?"

My heart races, and instinctively I reach for Viking. My hand brushes his, but I drop it. I've gotten by without him for four years. I won't reach for him now.

"Sounded like a tree. Must have taken out the power lines."

A soft glow illuminates his features, and then he flicks on his phone light. "I've got a better flashlight in my office."

I move toward the door with my hands out, bumping into desks as I go. There's another thump from outside, and I startle. My hip crashes against the side of a desk, and I stumble. Viking lunges forward to steady me, and our bodies collide chest to chest as his phone drops to the floor, plunging us into darkness.

I gasp as his arms wrap around me, cocooning me in a warm embrace that makes the storm feel far away. The scent of roasted malt, coffee, and the leather of his jacket cocoons me.

Heat radiates from his body, and the thumping of my heart is as loud as the rain hammering on the roof.

His thumb brushes my cheek, and his warm breath caresses my skin.

"Tell me to let you go," he whispers.

My mouth moves, but I can't form the words.

Our lips meet. And it's achingly slow, then hungry as years of longing explode to the surface. Lighting flashes above, illuminating our silhouettes against the wall followed by thunder rumbling overhead, which I feel all the way through my body.

Fluorescent lights crackle on, flooding the office with light. My eyes fly open, and I jerk backwards out of Viking's arms. My body is on fire from his touch and I stare up at the lights, trying to compose myself.

"The generator's kicked in."

Viking drops his hands to his sides, and his fingers clench as if he's lost something vital.

He steps forward. "Sydney, tell me what I have to do to make this right."

There's a pleading expression in his eyes, and it reminds me of that night when I left voicemails on his phone pleading for him to stay. A sharp pain of hurt fires in my chest, and I fold my arms over it.

"Nothing will make this right, Viking. You'll leave again. Just like last time."

He takes another step toward me, and I take a step back. If he gets too close, I might cave again. I might give in to what my body wants instead of what my head tells me I must do.

"I walked away once because I thought I was doing the right thing. I was wrong. I'm not leaving again."

His jaw works like he wants to say something more, but I don't give him the chance.

"Your intentions don't matter. Your actions do."

I swipe my purse from where I left it by my desk. "Storm or no storm, I'm driving home, because controlling how I leave is one thing I learned from you."

I stride toward the door, not daring to look him in the eyes. I make it out of the office when the lights flicker, and for a second time we're plunged into darkness.

I stay completely still. I'm not going to risk colliding with Viking again. If he kissed me a second time, I'm not sure I'd have the strength to walk away. But walk away is the only thing I can do to protect my heart.

I dig into my purse and find my phone at the same time that Viking gets his.

"The generator must have cut out."

That's not good news. "If the fermenting process is halted for too long, we'll lose the entire batch."

"I'll grab my flashlight and take a look."

I use the light from my phone to make sure I'm well clear of Viking as he moves past me to get to his office. Despite all my bravado, I won't leave him here on his own.

While he's in the office, my phone buzzes with a persistent alarm.

I frown at the emergency alert, and my heart sinks as I scan it.

Viking comes out of his office holding his phone up. "Did you get the alert?"

"Yes," I bite out.

Wild Heart Mountain is now under a severe thunderstorm warning. They've closed all the mountain roads and are issuing a shelter-in-place for at least the next six hours.

In the faint light from his phone, there's a ghost of a smile. "Looks like we're stuck here together, cupcake."

6

VIKING

*R*ain hammers the skylights as I sweep my flashlight beam over the wall of dead monitors. They must have shorted out with the power cut, which is no good if our thieves turn up tonight. Although I'm confident, no one will be out in this storm.

"I need to check the fermentation tanks." Sydney sounds worried, but at least she's still talking to me.

My lips tingle from the kiss we shared. The way she gave in to me for a few brief moments gives me hope. But right now, we need to get the generator up and running again, or we may as well drain the last few brews with the storm.

I take the lead with the flashlight as we head to the brewery floor.

Rain pounds the roof as I sweep my flashlight over the dead control panel for the fermentation tanks. The only light is the red flashing emergency light accompanied by the high-pitched screech of the alarm.

Sydney crouches next to the glycol pump and uses the light from her phone to take readings.

"The emergency battery works, so that's good news. But it only has seven minutes left."

She gets to her feet, and in the dim light I catch her worried expression.

"The generator's in the dockyard cage. Come on."

I use the flashlight to light the way as we jog across the brewery floor and slide open the heavy doors that lead to the loading bay.

Wind rattles the metal roller door that leads outside, and rain pummels the metal. The temperature is cooler in here, and there's only the roller door between us and the storm.

In the corner is the metal dockyard cage where the generator is. I grab my key chain from around my waist and fumble as I try to remember which key it is.

"Hold this." I hand Sydney the flashlight, and she shines it on the bunch of keys. The first one I try doesn't work. Nor does the second.

Sydney pulls out her phone and glances at the time. "We've got five minutes until the battery runs out."

The third key unlocks the cage, and I slide it open and step inside. Sydney squeezes in behind me, and I take the flashlight back while she holds up the light from her phone.

"The fuel tank shows half full." Sydney shouts to be heard over the wind battering the metal door.

My flashlight beam sweeps over the generator until I see the problem. A tripped coolant sensor.

"Hold the light," I shout back.

Sydney nods and takes the flashlight off me. There's a tool kit in the corner of the cage, and I grab a wrench and a screwdriver then edge back to the faulty sensor. My back's pressed against the metal of the cage, and there's just enough room to maneuver.

Sydney shimmies up close to me and angles the light on the sensor. The bolt is rusty, and it takes a few turns before I get it off.

The switch is blown, and it's not going to be a quick fix. The best I can do is bypass the switch and get the generator operational. After the storm, we'll need to fix it properly, but for now I rewire the switch and take it offline.

"Give that a try."

Sydney switches the main power, and the generator splutters to life. Lights in the loading bay flick on, and her face is illuminated in a smile.

"We did it!"

My grin matches her own.

With the generator working, we've saved the last six weeks of brewing. Sydney's stubbornness about not going home just saved the brewery a massive loss.

Her grin turns to a frown. "If a tree came down on the power lines, then it could be a while before the main line is restored."

"We'll turn off everything that's not necessary," I finish her thought. "So the power only goes to the tanks."

We lock the cage back up and switch off the loading bay lights as we go. Then we work through the building, turning off every light, computer, and snack machine.

The final stop is another check in on the control panel.

The flashing red light on the fermentation panel is a calm steady green, and the alarm has stopped. Sydney checks the fermentation levels and nods, satisfied.

"We'd better let Barrels know before he attempts to drive here and save the beer."

I fire off a text to Barrels letting him know the generator is working, and the beer is saved.

"I'd better let Nate know I'm safe."

As Sydney texts her brother, I stare at my blank phone. There's no one waiting for me at home. No one to worry if I'm stuck in the storm.

I slide my phone back in my pocket. It's been that way all my life. No point crying about it now.

A slice of lightning lights up the brewery floor, and the accompanying thunder shakes the building.

"Let's get to the cellar." I steer Sydney toward the stairs, and she doesn't brush my hand off her shoulder. "There's one small window. We'll be safe down there."

The thick stone walls block out the worst of the storm as we descend into the cellar. The rows of kegs loom in the darkness, picked up only by the beam of my flashlight.

"It's eerie down here in the dark."

Sydney shivers and crosses her arms over herself.

There's a wooden pallet in the corner, and I drag it to the middle of the floor and drape a drop cloth over it.

Sydney sinks into it and shivers. I slide my jacket off and drape it over her shoulders.

"Here. Take this."

She pulls it around her shoulders, getting lost inside.

"Wait here," I tell her. "I'll be back in a minute."

I return a few minutes later with a lantern I found in the staff room and the last mug of coffee. "Yours was empty and this is lukewarm."

I hold it out to her, and she takes a sip. Her shoulders drop, and for the first time the defensive expression is gone from her face.

"Thank you."

I nod once, listening to the wind howl through the vents. A long beat goes by.

"You deserve to know what happened. Why I re-enlisted. I wrote it to you in letters, but I guess you never read them.

I turn to her in the faint glow from the lantern. I can't see her expression. But she doesn't stop me, so I go on.

"Did I ever tell you about Tank? The guy I was in foster care with?"

There's a long silence. "You never told me anything about when you were in foster care."

She's right. Some things aren't worth talking about, or they're too painful. I never wanted to come across as complaining. Foster care sucks, but shit happens, and I got out of there and found myself a purpose in the army. There never seemed to be any point in talking about it. But perhaps I should have.

"Tank was in the same foster home as I was. The last one I was in before I aged out of the system."

I pause, remembering the bright-eyed kid with the wicked grin who could talk to anyone about anything while stealing their wallet from right under their noses.

"He was the closest thing I ever had to a brother. He was the smartest kid I ever knew, but he hated school. We enlisted at the same time. We did basic training together and were put in the same platoon. But we got separated on the second enlistment. It's not surprising the army saw his potential. He was trained in logistics; I was left in infantry."

I take a swig of coffee, wishing it was something stronger to dull the ache in my chest.

"Tank was killed by an IED in Iraq. It happened on my last leave."

Sydney stiffens beside me. My last leave was when we got close.

"While we were playing happy families, some fucker was making crude bombs to end his life."

I squeeze the coffee mug so tight my fingers hurt.

"I heard about his death on the final day of re-enlistment. He was my brother, Sydney. I had to go back to the fight. I had to honor him.

"I still wear his dog tags." I pull the metal from around my neck, and it catches in the dim light. I carry a piece of my brother with me every day.

Sydney stirs next to me, and I continue before she has time to cut me off.

"I hated the way I did it, with a letter. I thought there

would be time to see you, but because I'd left it to the last minute, I had to report straight to Fort Bragg. We were shipped out the next day."

"I would have waited for you."

Her words cut to my heart.

"I know. But I was cut up by his death. All I wanted was to get the fuckers who had ended his life, and I was ready to lay down my life to do it. I truly thought the only way I would be coming back was in a body bag. I didn't want you to have that grief. I thought it would be easier if you forgot about me."

There's silence between us, and I can hear Sydney breathing.

"I couldn't forget." Her voice is sad and tinged with bitterness. "No matter how far I ran, I couldn't forget you. We were supposed to do that trip together."

"I'm sorry, Sydney. I freaked out. We had all these plans. To travel, then to get a cabin back here on the mountain and start a family. But the truth is, when we talked about those things, it frightened me. I didn't know how I was going to provide all those things for you.

"I don't come from money, Sydney, and a soldier's wage can't support a family for long. I had no skills, and the club was only just starting up. I came from poverty, and I was scared I'd drag us both down there again."

She sighs. "You're fucking stupid, Viking. Do you think I don't want to work? It's the 21st century. You don't have to do it all on your own. I don't expect a man to support me."

The words hang in the air, and while I love Sydney's

43

independence, there's a big part of me that does want to support her. To take care of her and provide for her.

Her voice wavers. "You left for honor and money, and you didn't give me a vote."

I slide my arm around her shoulders, wanting to ease the hurt that I caused.

"I still want that cabin in the woods, Sydney, with you. I saved hard and I learned carpentry. I can build it myself with help from the guys. I don't deserve a second chance, but if you want to give me one, it will be on your terms."

She shuffles on the pallet, but she doesn't move away or wiggle out from under my arm.

"Dreams change; people change."

The generator hums through the concrete, and I keep my arm firmly around her. If she gives me a second chance, I'm never letting her go.

7

SYDNEY

a noise startles me awake. The lantern has dimmed and the generator's distant hum has slowed. I blink slowly and rub my fingers into my stiff neck.

I must have fallen asleep next to Viking, the exhaustion of the storm finally catching up with me. But the pallet is cold and empty now. His jacket is still draped over me, and the empty coffee mug sits on the concrete floor.

There's a muffled clank from nearby, and I turn to the sound. Viking's silhouette is framed against the door that leads to the loading bay. He presses his ear to it, listening.

I pad quietly over to him and he leans down to whisper in my ear, his hot breath tickling my skin.

"I heard something. I'm going to check it out."

He starts to move away, but I pull him back, my fingers catching in his hair. "Who would be out in the storm?"

He's thinking about the missing kegs, but it's unlikely anyone would come for them now, not with the roads closed. His lips brush my ear, sending heat through me that thaws the cold in my bones.

"Someone desperate."

The door that leads to the loading bay is in the corner near a stack of shelves and the seller control panel. Viking silently edges it open and slides through. Halfway he pauses and puts a palm out when I start to follow. He points two fingers to his eyes and then toward the cellar floor—military hand signals I remember from years ago. A surge of nostalgia rattles through me, and I nod, staying behind the doorjamb.

The only illumination in the dockyard is the faint glow coming through the high windows. A shadow moves across the dockyard floor, and I slap a hand over my mouth to stifle a gasp. Another shadow joins the first, this one smaller and hunched over. I don't see Viking, but I know he must be there, silently moving in on the intruders.

I edge away from the door to the control panel, ready to switch on the lights if Viking needs me to.

The shadows move closer to the door. My heartbeat quickens. I hear the squeak of rubber soles on concrete.

It's obvious they know their way around, and they're heading for the cellar where I'm hiding.

One shadow swings something by his side, and metal glints in the dim light. A bolt cutter.

I grope for a weapon, anything I can use. I reach around the shelving unit, and my hand closes on a screwdriver. I raise it to shoulder height, ready to use it if I have to.

They're almost at the door when a shape blocks my view.

"Easy, fellas."

Viking's steady voice eases my pounding heart. The intruders stop. One of them lifts the bolt cutter like a bat.

"Set it down, nice and easy." Viking raises his hands to show he's unarmed. "No one's going to get hurt."

The figure pauses, and while he hesitates Viking lunges forward and grabs his wrist. With a quick twist the bolt cutters drop to the floor, and Viking pins the intruder's arm behind his back. The second intruder backs up and into a stack of empty kegs which rattle, and one falls over and rolls across the floor.

I flip the lights on, and the intruders blink in the bright light. For the first time I see they're just kids, teenagers barely out of school.

Their shoes are soaked from the storm, their over-sized hoodies dripping onto the concrete. They're shivering, their cheeks blotched with rain and fear.

They look familiar. Then it hits me: They've been on a tour through here.

"We just needed someplace dry," the older boy says.

Viking still has his arm pinned, but gently, keeping him in check without pain. I step out from behind the door. I don't want to get too close, so I stretch my booted foot out and slide the bolt cutter toward me, then bend to pick it up. The younger boy darts a glance my way and I stand tall; the bolt cutter gripped in my hands.

"Are there any more of you?" Viking asks.

"No." The older one shakes his head. "Just us."

"You've been here before," I say. "You've done the tour."

The boy looks down, silent.

"What are the bolt cutters for?" Viking asks quietly.

They don't answer.

"I've got security cameras," he says, "and some missing kegs. The footage shows you two taking them."

It's a bluff, but the boys don't know the security cameras have been out of action until a few days ago.

The boys glance at each other, fear bright in their eyes.

The smaller one hisses to the older one, "I thought you took care of the cameras."

The older boy shrugs, shooting him a dirty look. "Don't say anything."

"Who are you stealing the kegs for?" Viking's voice softens.

The younger boy hangs his head. "We just needed extra money, for shoes and stuff. We didn't mean any harm."

"How many have you taken?" Viking already knows the answer, but he's testing their honesty.

"Just two," the older boy mumbles.

Viking releases his grip, and the boy rubs his wrist.

"You picked the wrong night," Viking says.

The boy shrugs. "We figured no one would be out. The roads are closed."

I peer at the boys, wondering at their desperate situation. What would drive them out here in a storm, risking their lives for a hundred bucks?

"There's an alert in place. Did you know that?" Viking asks.

The boy shrugs. "We need the money."

I share a look with Viking. In his eyes, I see his past. He was this boy once.

"You picked the wrong night," he repeats softly, "but maybe not the wrong people."

His gaze remains on me, and there's compassion in his eyes. He raises his eyebrows at me. Compassion is what's needed here, not discipline. I nod and lower the bolt cutters.

"Let's talk someplace warm."

The kids exchange wary looks. Viking shepherds them toward the cellar door, and I follow them upstairs to the office.

8

VIKING

I march the two rain-soaked teens up the stairs and into the staff room. Sydney flicks on the lights as we go. She starts a pot of filter coffee, the machine drip-feeding slowly, then leans against the counter with her arms folded, watching the two boys.

The tall one is lean. Dark hair hangs into his eyes. His hoodie is far too big, and he pulls the cuffs down to cover his hands. He looks at the floor, at the table—everywhere but at me.

"Take a seat, boys."

They drag out chairs with a scrape against the vinyl floor and sit, hunched over in the plastic chairs. I crouch so I'm at their eye level.

"My name's Chris Erikson, but people call me Viking. What are your names?"

The smaller one flicks a glance at the older before whispering, "I'm Marcus. People call me Mouse."

"I'm Rio," the tall one adds.

"Rio and Marcus. How old are you?"

"I'm seventeen," Rio says.

"I'll be seventeen in two weeks," Marcus murmurs.

He's small for his age, and scrawny. The fact that he stresses he's almost seventeen tells me he has something to prove.

"We only wanted two kegs to sell," Rio blurts. "We sell them to people staying at the campground. There's always someone looking for a party."

"We need cash for sneakers," Marcus adds. "The group home doesn't cover extras."

The words hit hard. I remember what it was like, me and Tank running around, stealing bikes and selling them so we could buy boots and a winter coat. You do what it takes to survive. I rub the scar on my temple. This could have been me and Tank a few years ago.

"I get it," I say quietly. "I grew up in rotation, too."

The boys lift their eyes, surprised.

"But stealing kegs will only lead to trouble. It won't fix your worn-out shoes in the long run."

Sydney draws a slow breath at my confession, and when I glance at her, there's compassion in her gaze. I give her a small smile, then turn back to the boys.

Both our phones buzz suddenly, as does one buried deep in Rio's hoody. I ignore mine while Sydney checks hers.

"The roads are open again," she says. "The storm has been downgraded, and we're back to a watch."

Rio pulls out his phone, and it's an old model with a

cracked screen. He stares at the alert then puts his phone on the table.

"How did you get here?" I ask.

They glance at each other. "We drove."

I raise a brow. "Whose car?"

"We borrowed it from the group home," Rio admits.

"Do they know you borrowed it?"

He looks down. "No," he says quietly. "We'll get it back."

Call me soft, but I believe him. A car is a precious resource, and they might need it again.

"Okay, so you can get home. Here's what we're going to do."

I take out my phone and snap Rio's picture.

He scowls at me. "What did you do that for?"

I don't answer. I photograph Marcus, then the two of them together.

"Syd, got a notebook?" She heads to the office and returns with one and two pens.

I set the paper on the table and hand over the pens. "Write your full names, dates of birth, placement address."

Rio takes a pen warily; I wait while they write.

"You're coming back here Monday morning at nine o'clock sharp. You'll work off the kegs you stole, then we'll talk about legit jobs and what you want to do with your futures. If you're not here at nine, these pictures go straight to the sheriff."

I scroll to Badge's number and show it to them, my finger covering the digits.

"The sheriff is a good buddy of mine. In fact, he owns part of this brewery. He won't be happy about people stealing from him. Be here at nine."

They hand over the page, and my eyes soften when I read the placement: *Denning House.* Mrs. Denning was the last foster stop for me and Tank.

"Mrs. Denning kept me alive once. Tell her Viking says hello, and I'll come visit her soon."

I stand up. "I know how the system works, boys. If you run, I'll find you. You know who owns this brewery? The Wild Riders Motorcycle Club. We're all veterans, which means we're tough motherfuckers and we have a vast and far reaching network. Make the right call."

Sydney comes over and hands each boy an energy bar from the vending machine. "The roads are open but drive safe."

She catches my eye. For the first time, I feel like we're truly a team.

I walk the kids to the door. The rain has eased to a steady drizzle. I watch until they climb into their beat-up sedan and the taillights disappear down the mountain. Only then do I lock the door.

Back in the kitchen, Sydney pours two cups of coffee. "That was impressive."

I let out a long breath. "I'm just paying it forward. Someone gave me a chance once. Sometimes that's all these kids need."

She nods slowly. "You did good, Viking."

Her praise means more than she'll ever know.

9

SYDNEY

*M*y fingers tap on the fermenter control panel. The levels have stayed within range, which is a relief. The main power came back on ten minutes ago, and we're doing a final check before heading home.

When I turn around, Viking is watching me, his heated gaze sending sparks skittering through my body.

"I meant what I said earlier," I remind him. "That was a good thing you did—how you dealt with those boys."

He shrugs. "It felt like the right thing."

Viking has always done what feels right. I understood why he re-enlisted four years ago, even though it hurt. If he'd stayed, he would have regretted not honoring his friend, and it would have poisoned our relationship.

I didn't get it then, but I do now.

"Let's lock up downstairs," he says.

I follow Viking down to the cellar and through to the

docking bay where we find a small window propped open.

The boys explained that they'd noticed it during the tour and spotted where the security cameras were. Marcus, the smaller one, hid behind kegs, and when no one was around, he climbed up to the window and wedged a piece of wood in it to leave it ajar. Just wide enough to get his hand in from the outside and force it open.

Viking climbs onto the shelves to remove the wedge.

If they'd fallen, it could have been serious. It shows how desperate they were.

We secure the window, switch off the lights, and move through to the cellar, locking the door behind us.

Back in the cellar, the cool air smells of dark oak, hops, and lingering rain. While Viking drags the pallet to its spot between the rows, I wander along the rows at the back of the cellar, where they keep the special barrels. The ones sealed in oak and aged longer to sell at a premium.

The scent of damp oak and vanilla surrounds me, and I run my hand over the rough wood and breathe deeply.

There are footsteps behind me, and when I turn Viking is closer than I expected. So close I catch the scent of leather and coffee that has me breathing deeply and wanting him closer.

My heartbeat thumps erratically as he stands before me, his gaze penetrating mine. His arm lifts, hesitating, but this time I reach for him first, clasping his hands in mine.

"I keep thinking about how you were with those kids," I whisper.

He lifts my hand to his mouth, brushing my skin with his lips and making my pulse quicken.

"You're a good man, Viking."

He lowers my hand and places both his palms on my hips, guiding me backward until I bump against an oak barrel. My body bumps up against his hard one, and I gasp as heat zaps through my body. My head feels thick with him and hazy as he leans closer.

His mouth finds my neck, and I tilt my head and close my eyes as his warm lips trace slowly from my throat to my ear.

"Tell me to stop," he murmurs.

I open my eyes and shake my head. "I don't want you to stop."

His eyes flash with longing, and his lips claim mine. A sigh escapes me as I surrender to his kiss. One hand traces my collarbone while the other cups the back of my head, drawing me closer.

He steps forward, pressing me to the barrel so I have nowhere to go. And I don't want to go anywhere. I don't want anything but more of this, more of *him*.

His hands slide down my back, then lower until he cups my ass.

"There's my cupcakes," he growls, the once-infuriating nickname now a spark that ignites my need for him.

I thrust my hips, grinding against him, and his hands

skim down my leather skirt, gripping the hem, as he slowly hikes it up.

"Tell me to stop," his voice rasps, but he keeps lifting until the skirt bunches at my waist.

"Don't stop."

He groans into my mouth and his fingers slip under my stockings, peeling them down.

I'm panting hard as I come up for air, my lips swollen and my body on fire.

I shove his jacket off, sliding my fingertips beneath his T-shirt to feel the hard planes of his chest.

"I've missed this, cupcake," Viking confesses. "Missed you so damn much."

His hand slides between my legs, and I moan as he cups my heat.

"I missed this," he says again. "I missed all of you. I'm so sorry, Sydney."

I tug his T-shirt over his head, and in the dim light I drink in his muscles. My hands roam over his biceps and chest, making my fingertips tingle.

"I was mad at you, Viking. So fucking mad."

"I'm sorry."

I channel that anger, yanking open his jeans and shoving his boxers down. His dick springs free.

"I threw your dried daisies into the compost," I confess as I grip his length in my palms.

Viking groans, and his eyes flutter shut. I watch him battle for control as I hold him in my hand. His eyelids spring open, and his look is pure hunger.

He grips my stockings and rips them away with a hard yank.

"I still have the panties I ripped off you the last time we made love," he murmurs against my ear.

With another tug, my panties tear away in his hands.

I'm left in my knee-high boots and a bunched-up skirt, exposed and aching.

Heat floods me, and I cry out as his fingertips trail my most sensitive places.

"I never stopped loving you, Sydney."

He knocks my hand away and grips his length and slides it along my slickness.

"We were supposed to do that trip together," he groans. "But you took off before I had a chance to speak to you."

His tip nudges inside me, and my body quivers with anticipation.

"I know. I'm not sorry—" The rest of my sentence dissolves into a moan as he thrusts inside me.

My thighs widen to take him fully and I arch my back, leaning my elbows on the back of the barrel. It rocks backwards, and Viking grabs my hips to steady us.

"I found a hair tie of yours when I was deployed," he pants. "And wore it around my wrist the whole time I was in Afghanistan."

He lifts me, seating me on the barrel and driving deeper. I wrap my legs around his waist, the leather of my boots pressing into him.

He nuzzles into my neck, and his teeth graze my skin.

"I can't smell this scent without thinking of you," he breathes.

Words fail me as he moves, his hands cupping my ass. Memories crash over me—every time he made me feel beautiful, calling my too-soft backside his pair of cupcakes.

Viking thrusts deeper, and his movements become more frantic. My hips thrust to meet his, and my fingers dig into his shoulders. I let the sensation wash over me and surrender to him, truly surrender.

Years of hurt slip away as I remember how good we fit together, how much I loved him, how much I still do.

"I kept all your letters," I gasp.

Viking stills for a beat, and he leans back to look at me.

"You read my letters?" he rasps out.

"More than once."

He pulls me toward him, and this time it's slow. His kisses snake down my throat as he glides inside me.

"I love you, Sydney."

Pressure builds inside me, and with his words, I shatter. My nails dig into his shoulders, and I release four years of need as I cry his name.

He growls against my throat and shudders, pulling me tight towards him.

We cling to each other for a long beat. His forehead rests on mine, our breaths and heartbeats syncing.

"On long nights in the desert, this is what kept me going—thinking about this."

Gently, he lowers me from the barrel and pulls my skirt down. I steady myself, brushing a soft kiss over the scar on his forehead.

I ignore the warning in my head and give in to my heart.

"We can make new memories," I whisper. "Together."

10

VIKING

*A*s the clock above the bar in the tasting room rolls over to nine o'clock, I watch the door with my arms folded across my chest. Footsteps sound outside, the handle turns, and the door pushes open as Rio and Marcus shuffle inside.

My gaze flicks to the clock. They're right on time. A smile curls the corners of my mouth.

"Good morning, boys."

They murmur their greetings. They're in the same clothes they wore on Saturday night, but this time they're dry.

"This is the front door of the brewery. From now on, this is how you come and go. Got it?"

They both nod.

"If you earn our trust and want to keep working here, someday you might get a staff pass that will let you in the staff entrance. But trust has to be earned."

Rio scowls and shoves his hands into his pockets, and

I wonder if I've made a mistake. Too late to change course now.

"Right. Follow me, boys. We're going to see the boss."

They exchange frightened glances as I lead them onto the brewery floor. The floor is alive with activity while a new brew gets underway. Workers have been here since five o'clock this morning, and the smell of fresh hops hangs heavy in the air. Arlo and Hops are chatting by one of the tanks, and they give me a curious look. Up on the mezzanine, Sydney watches with her hands on her hips.

We head up the metal stairs, and I march the boys into Barrels's office. He sits behind a wooden desk, stony-faced, channeling his former army sergeant days. The boys shuffle in behind me, and I don't offer them a seat.

Barrel's leans forward. "What's this?"

"I caught your thieves."

His eyes narrow, and he reaches for his phone. "I'll get Badge."

The boys share a frightened look, and Marcus's eyes dart toward the door.

I raise a hand. "Hear me out, Barrels. I've got a better idea."

Barrels sits back in his chair with his arms crossed. "Start talking."

With some encouragement, I get Rio talking. As he explains the keg scheme and their reasons for it, Barrels frown deepens. He didn't grow up in foster care like I did.

When Rio gets to the part about prying open the

window, Barrels slams a fist on the desk, but before he erupts, I cut in.

"They're here to repay the brewery, starting today."

"Those kegs are worth a lot of money," Barrels counters. "How will they repay when they can't even afford shoes?"

"They'll work it off."

Barrels eyes the kids. "Two kegs. A week of hard labor. Nine to five Monday through Saturday."

Both boys nod.

"You give me a week of work, we forget about it," Barrels says. "Disrespect us, and you don't get a second chance."

The boys nod again.

"There's debris from the storm to clean up," Barrels continues. "You'll be sweeping and cleaning and scrubbing. Some barrels got knocked about. I want every dent buffed out. Understand?"

"Yes," they both mutter.

I open the door for them, and they shuffle onto the mezzanine.

"Wait here," I tell them and duck back into the office, closing the door behind me.

Barrels folds his arms, but there's an amused look on his face. "It's a good thing you're doing, Viking. But they're your responsibility. If another keg walks out, I'll hold you accountable."

"Understood, boss."

I only hope I've made the right call. Everyone deserves a second chance.

. . .

A few hours later, I head to the loading dock. Water sloshes across the floor as Rio wrestles with the power washer. Every time he pulls the trigger, the pressure nearly knocks him over.

"Hold it like this." I demonstrate. "Point it down so it gets the whole floor."

"Yes, sir." He adjusts his angle, surprising me with the crisp reply.

"It's almost one. You guys eaten yet?"

They shake their heads.

"Not hungry," Marcus mumbles, which I take to mean they don't have any lunch.

"I'll be back soon. Then I'll show you where the staff room is."

Twenty minutes later, I return with sandwiches Maggie rustled up and two chocolate-chip cookies. The boys' eyes go wide. These are probably the first cookies they've had in a long time.

In the staff room their eyes shift less, and they seem more relaxed than I've seen them.

"You guys still in school?"

Rio shakes his head. "Nah, just finished."

Marcus look sideways, and I wonder what the whole story is here.

"What'll you do for work?"

They shrug. "Don't know," Rio says.

"Ever considered the military?"

They shake their heads, but interest flickers in Rio's eyes.

"This brewery is run by veterans. The military gives you discipline, purpose, and a steady paycheck. It saved me when I came out of foster care."

"Don't you have to go to war?" Marcus asks, wiping mayonnaise from his mouth.

I chuckle at his concern. "Sure, if there's a war on. You sign up to protect your country. It's a noble cause."

"I've heard training's really hard," Rio says, leaning in.

"It's tough, probably the toughest thing you'll ever do, but it's worth it. You learn what you can endure and take pride in yourself. The military saved my life; it could save yours."

I glance up and find Sydney leaning against the doorframe watching us. The smile on her lips makes me forget what I was saying.

I push back my chair and stand.

"Think you can find your own way back to the loading dock?"

They nod. I clap Rio's shoulder, then Marcus's.

"Show up every day, earn trust."

I stride over to Sydney and step right up close so I can smell her perfume. Memories of two nights ago against the barrel flash through my mind. My eyes drop to her lips, and I twirl a strand of her hair in my fingers.

"You must be due for a few hours off. Come for a ride with me."

. . .

Ten minutes later, I am on my bike with Sydney on the back heading up the mountain. A stillness settles over the peaks. You'd never know a storm ripped through only a few days ago.

With Sydney's hands clasped around my waist, I can't help the grin on my face: fresh mountain air, my bike between my thighs, and my woman at my back. I have a second chance at life—at this life—and I won't let it go.

We ride for twenty minutes up the mountain, enjoying the wind on my face, with no destination in mind. A fire road leads off the main road and I take it, searching for a secluded spot. The path narrows, but the bike handles it. We weave through the trees and stop in a hidden glade. Leaves carpet the ground, and sun glints through the canopy.

I keep the engine running, enjoying the soft hum of the bike. Sliding off, I unhook our helmets and dangle them over the handlebars. My hands stay on Sydney's hips, unable to let her go now that I have her in my grasp again. My hand slides down her back, over her perfect ass.

"I can't stop thinking about the other night," I murmur. "About you."

"Neither can I."

My mouth captures hers as I press her against the warm seat. Insects hum in the trees as I unzip her skirt, peeling it down thick thighs, and kneel in the dirt before her.

"You're so beautiful, Sydney."

I nudge her legs apart and kiss her stomach. She gasps when the engine's vibration reaches her.

"Viking, the bike's still on."

I give her a wicked grin. "I know."

My lips caress her thighs, and I gently pull her panties aside. Her scent floods me, and I breathe deeply. The deep purr of the engine makes her vibrate under my tongue. Hands tangle in my hair as she throws her legs over my shoulders, the leather of her boots sliding against my neck.

She giggles until my mouth covers her sweet pussy, and laughter turns to a gasp. Her leg goes wide, and the heel of her boot presses into my clavicle. Pain shoots through me, heating my blood. My tongue laps faster as her heel digs deeper, and I bury my face in her until she cries my name, her moans echoing through the forest.

I don't wait for her tremors to fade. I unzip and free my cock. Her wild eyes meet mine before our lips crash together.

She guides me inside and wraps her legs tight around me. One hand grips the handlebar, the other the back of the bike, while I thrust. Heat envelops me, but it is not enough, will never be enough with Sydney.

I clasp her thighs and pull her legs over my shoulders so the leather of her boots skims my neck, and I drive in deeper.

"Sydney." Her name is a prayer on my lips.

Four years of hurt and regret pour out with every thrust. Her head falls back as I rub her clit hard and fast until she shatters and I let go, exploding with her.

"Viking!" she screams.

Our cries send a flock of birds into the sky.

Breathless, I finally kill the engine, and she plants her boots on the forest floor.

"I'm going to smell like gas," she mutters.

"I'm going to smell like you," I tell her. "Totally worth it."

I slide my arms around her waist, resting my forehead against hers.

"This is me staying, Syd."

She gives a non-committal harrumph, and a smile teases her lips. She's finally starting to believe me.

SYDNEY

*B*y Friday we've slipped into an easy routine. Viking brings me coffee in the morning, and when we can we spend our lunch break taking a ride up the mountain. But this morning I want to surprise him.

It's early when I punch in the security code and let myself into the brewery. The brew team has been here since dawn, but the office area is silent and dark. My purse is slung over my shoulder, and in my hands I carry the cardboard box that Maggie left for me in the club-room kitchen.

Balanced on top is a mug of coffee from Davis, black, no sugar, the way Viking likes it.

The door to the security hub is closed, and I place my goodies down on the ground and use my ID card to gain access. Propping the door open with my hip, I pick up the box and the mug. I glance down the walkway, but there's no sign of Viking. As planned, I've timed it so he's doing his morning rounds downstairs.

Inside his office is a wall of monitors. The extra cameras show every inch of the brewery. My cheeks heat as I realize that what we did a week ago against the barrels will be on record. I bet Viking hasn't forgotten. I'll have to remind him to erase it. Although knowing him, he's probably saved himself a copy somewhere private.

I smile at the thought, and heat surges through my body. Since I surrendered to Viking, I can't get enough of him.

I place the cardboard box down on the desk, pushing a notebook and Viking's phone out of the way. Inside the box are two round cupcakes. They're decorated in a thick layer of frosted pink icing with black sprinkles. I leave the lid down and put the mug next to the box.

I'm about to sneak away when his phone buzzes on the desk. It vibrates so hard it makes the box move.

I peer at the screen: *Unknown INTL*

Who would be calling Viking from overseas?

I glance up at the bank of screens and spot Viking in the docking bay talking with Barrels. There's a shipment going out today, and the loading bay is alive with activity.

The phone rings out, and I tell myself it's none of my business.

I adjust the box so it's square on the desk and pick my purse up off the floor.

The phone buzzes again, and it's the same unknown overseas number.

It could be one of his military buddies who's still

enlisted. My hand hovers over the phone, unsure. If something has happened, he'll want to know.

I pick it up and answer.

"Mr. Erikson?" The voice is female with a Middle Eastern lilt.

I'm too stunned to tell her that I'm not him, but she takes my silence as assent and continues.

"Mr. Johnstone is thrilled to have you onboard."

She rattles on before I have a chance to stop her.

"Your transport departs next Monday at 0800 hours. Bring desert gear, and the rest will be provided."

My body freezes. "Transport..." My voice comes out in a whisper, and the woman on the phone doesn't hear because she keeps talking.

"The paperwork will follow in a secure email."

Cold spreads from my fingertips, turning my body to ice. Viking is leaving.

"He's not here right now," I manage to get out. My words are clipped. "I'll pass on the message."

"We're thrilled to have him with us," she gushes.

I end the call and throw the phone down on the desk in front of me. I take a step back as if it might burn me.

Viking's leaving again. Just like I knew he would.

I've been so stupid to believe he meant to stay this time. I should have listened to my head not my heart.

I glance up at the screens, and Viking isn't at the loading dock. I pick him up walking through the brewery floor. He's on his way back up here, and I really don't want to see the duplicitous asshole.

I grab the box off his desk, not caring as it tips side-

71

ways and there's the sound of two cupcakes sliding together.

I grab the mug of coffee and my purse and stride back to the staff entrance.

I pull open the door and jog down the steps. There's a line of trash cans by the entrance, and I lift he lid off the first one I see and dump the box of cupcakes inside.

Then I get in my car, and with shaky hands drive out of the parking lot and away from the man who still has the power to break my heart.

12
VIKING

"That's the last of the pale ales," Rio shouts over the beeping of the forklift as it reverses away from the truck.

He waves a clipboard at Barrels, who scrutinizes his work before slapping him on the back and giving him a curt nod, which is the highest form of praise anyone's going to get from the ex-sergeant.

Without being told, Marcus grabs the wooden broom from the corner and sweeps the area where dust has built up where the kegs were aging.

I smile at the boys. They were here before nine this morning to help with the loading of the delivery. They've more than paid back the stolen kegs, and I'll speak to Barrels about a bonus. Enough to get them the shoes they need.

With the boys under Barrels watch, I head up to the office.

I'm thinking about Sydney and wondering what she'll

be wearing today. I hope it's her leather skirt. And of course it will be the knee-high boots she lives in.

I hum to myself as I stride across the metal walkway to the office. But when I look in, Sydney's desk is empty. Not only empty, but her computer is also off and her purse isn't by her desk.

That's unusual.

Isla is the only other person in the office today. We haven't announced to the club yet that we're dating, but you'd have to be blind not to realize something's going on between us.

Isla looks up from her desk. "She called in sick."

I frown at her words and reach for my phone, but it's not in my pocket. I must have left it on my desk this morning.

I find it in my office and send a quick text to Sydney.

Not like you to call in sick. U ok?

I tap the side of my phone, waiting for a reply.

Three little dots appear, but no text comes through.

On the cameras I spy Barrels coming up the walkway stairs, and I head to the corridor to cut him off.

"I heard Sydney called in sick today."

He keeps walking, and I fall into step beside him. "That's right. I hope it isn't catching; I don't need you going down too."

His mouth tugs up in a smile, but I'm not in the mood for jokes.

"It's not like Syd to call in sick."

Barrels frowns. "She hasn't had a sick day since she started. Did she seem sick to you?"

I press my lips together. I don't want to tell the boss that Sydney seemed fine when I drove her up the mountain after work last night and made love to her pressed up against a tree.

"Maybe she needs a mental health day," I mumble.

"Maybe she needs to get away from you." Barrels smirks as he claps me on the shoulder, but his words make me uneasy.

"Your boys are working out good." He pauses outside his office. "They've paid off the kegs and I'd love to keep them on, but we just don't have enough work for two of them full time."

"I've got an idea," I say. "Something that might interest them."

"Good. It was a good thing you did, Viking, giving those boys a chance."

He slaps me on the shoulder and disappears into his office.

I pull out my phone and call Sydney's number. It goes straight to voicemail, and my jaw tightens.

I leave a message saying I hope she feels better and asking her to call me. But I can't help the nagging feeling that something isn't right.

. . .

The sunset glows on the wet asphalt as I ride down the mountain and to Sydney's place. Despite numerous texts and calls throughout the day, I haven't heard from her.

Uneasiness grips my gut as I park outside the huge cabin that belongs to Sydney's brother. It's more like a mansion than a cabin with three stories and a turret room. It sits on a ridge with forest surrounding it on three sides and a dramatic clifftop drop on the other.

This is not the type of cabin I'll be able to provide for Sydney. My heart sinks. Perhaps she's realized my limitations. That I'll never be able to provide for her in this way.

A small cabin in the woods with her and our family is all I need, but maybe Sydney needs more.

As I pull my helmet off, I glance up at the turret windows where Sydney told me she's staying. The curtains are pulled closed.

It's with a twisted stomach that I push the smart doorbell. I'm positive Nate's staring at my face on his on-screen app, so I run a hand through my hair and try not to look anxious.

The door opens, and I'm greeted by Nate. He's got his hands folded over his chest, showing off his muscular forearms. For a computer geek, he's one of the buffest guys I know.

"She doesn't want to see you."

His words confirms the fear that's been growing in my stomach all day.

"She's not sick, is she?"

Nate's look is thunderous. "Whatever you did, stay away from my sister."

We might be MC brothers, but blood is thicker when it comes to family.

"I just want to talk to her."

He steps forward so his bulk takes up the entire door frame. "Sydney might appear tough Viking, but underneath her armor is a big heart. You broke it once; I won't let you break it again."

He takes a step inside and closes the door. Before it can shut, I put my hand in the door frame.

"But I don't know what I've done. Just let me talk to her."

Nate shakes his head. "Just leave, Viking. It's what you're good at."

I release my hand, and the door clicks shut. Panic grips me, and my hands shake. I don't know what has spooked Sydney. Maybe she's realized I'll never give a life like this, but how will I know if I can't talk to her?

Gathering a handful of pebbles from the gravel drive, I take a step backward until I can see the turret windows.

I throw a pebble, and it makes a loud plunk as it hits glass.

The next one is louder, and if I have to break one of Nate's windows to see her I damn well will.

I throw another pebble, then another before the curtain pulls back and Sydney's angry face appears at the glass. She pulls the window open.

"Go away, Chris."

Her eyebrows draw together, and her eyes flash with anger. It's like the last few weeks never happened.

"What's wrong, Syd? What did I do?"

"I know about the job. I know you're leaving."

I stare up at her, trying to make sense of what she's saying. "What job?"

She shakes her head. "Don't try and deny it. Your transport leaves next Monday. I'll work from home until then so I don't have to see you. Just go."

She must mean the Middle Eastern gig that Paulie's convinced I'm going to say yes to. But I haven't said yes.

"I'm not taking the job."

She shakes her head. "Unbelievable. Still lying to me. I took the call, Chris. I know you're going. Now just go."

The window slams shut and the curtain tugs closed and settles into stillness.

I grab my phone and scroll through the missed calls. There's an unknown international number from this morning, and it says I spoke to them for almost a minute.

"Fuck."

"It's not what you think," I call out.

But the window stays closed and the curtains stay drawn.

13

VIKING

I pull the club van up to the curb outside the address that Rio and Marcus gave me for their group home. The front door slams open, and Rio jogs down the steps followed by Marcus. Rio has cut his hair short so it no longer falls over his eyes, and they're both wearing collared shirts. Rio's hangs baggy on his thin shoulders, and Marcus's is too tight.

My lips curl up in a smile. They've tried.

I unlock the passenger door for them, and they both slide in.

It's a short drive to the nearest army recruitment center in Hope, and the boys mostly sit in nervous silence.

I pull up outside the gray building, and we get out of the van. Posters of boot camp line the walls and the boys jostle each other, making jokes to hide their nervousness.

We come to the office for the army, and a gruff voice answers my knock. I open the door, and behind a large wooden desk sits a thick man in army fatigues. He stands up when we enter, and his terse expression breaks into a grin.

"Viking." He comes out from behind the desk to shake my hand and slaps me on the back. "I haven't seen you in years."

"It's been a while." His handshake is as bone-crushingly firm as I remember.

"Sergeant Mallory, I've bought you a couple of recruits."

The sergeant gives the boys a once-over and nods his head. "What's your name?"

"Rio, sir." Rio stands up straight, and Marcus does the same. I feel a surge of pride.

The sergeant gives a nod of approval. "Why do you want to join up?"

Marcus shrugs. "Not much else to do."

The sergeant's gaze meets mine. I was once a boy just like this, with no future and no prospects.

"That's as good a reason as any," murmurs the sergeant.

He hands them the paperwork, and I stand in the corner while they fill it out. Pride mingles with worry as they sign their lives over to the military.

There are worse things for them, I tell myself. Rio is like an excited kid asking questions while Marcus is quieter, but his sharp eyes miss nothing.

"Meet me back here tomorrow, and we'll get your uniforms," the sergeant tells them. "Ones that fit."

The boys talk excitedly as I drop them back at home. Before they get out of the van, I clap Rio on the shoulder.

"When you've had enough of military life, come back and see us. The MC is for veterans, and if you like bikes and beer, it's not a bad club to belong to. You'll find brotherhood in the army, and when you can't do that anymore, there's brotherhood in the MC."

Marcus gives me a rare smile. "Thank you."

Rio grins at me. "Appreciate what you did. No one's ever done something like that for me before."

I shake both of their hands solemnly, seeing the ghosts of myself and Tank all those years ago. "Look out for each other and keep out of trouble. The military doesn't mess around with discipline."

"Yes, sir."

They scamper into the house and I watch them go, feeling like a proud parent.

Before I pull away, I slide my phone out of my pocket. There are no messages from Sydney, and I fire her a quick text.

We need to talk cupcake

As I'm staring at my phone waiting for the double ticks to appear, it vibrates with a call from Paulie.

"I'm sorry about my office contacting you. I added your name to the list, but it was supposed to say unconfirmed."

I can't keep the irritation out of my voice. "It's still a no, Paulie."

"Come on, what's keeping you on that mountain of yours? You haven't got family, and last I heard there was no Mrs. Viking."

I'm silent. He's right. Without Sydney, there's no reason to stay.

Paulie sighs. "The truth is, it's hard to find decent guys. I trust you, Viking, and I can't say that about many people. I'll double the offer. One six-month contract and life-changing money."

I close my eyes. Life-changing money could get me that cabin. But what good is it if Sydney doesn't want me?

It was too much expecting to come back here and earn her forgiveness. I blew things with her. I broke her heart, and she'll never trust me again. And without Sydney, what reason do I have to stay?

"Look, I'm coming up your way this weekend," Paulie says. "I'll stop in and we can talk in person."

"All right," I agree. "I'll see you then."

14

SYDNEY

The clubroom buzzes with conversation as I twirl the pasta salad with my fork.

"You going to eat that or play with it?" Nate nudges me with his elbow, and my fork skitters across my plate. It lands on the edge of my plate, and a piece of pasta rolls off it and onto the table.

"Play with it."

My neck prickles, and I glance up to find Viking staring at me from across the room. He has a pitcher of ale in one hand and looks as miserable as I feel.

But I'm not going to let him see that.

I sit up straight and scoop a forkful of pasta into my mouth. I turn to my brother and force a smile as I chew the pasta and swallow it down with a large gulp of wine.

Nate says something about a new kind of coffee bean he's trying and I laugh loudly, earning a confused look from my bother. But damned if I'll let Viking see he's hurt me again.

I worked from home all week, feigning a lingering cold. But I couldn't miss the club dinner.

It must only be a few days until Viking leaves, and then I can get back to my life. My lonely life.

I push the thought from my head and try for another mouthful of pasta.

The front door to the restaurant bursts open, and a man I don't recognize strides in. He's wearing tan chinos and heavy boots, and his hair's cut in a buzz-cut.

Obviously military, but by the murmurs that ripple around the room, I'd say he's not an expected guest.

The man strides straight over to Viking followed by a woman in camo pants and a headscarf.

"You're a hard man to track down." The stranger's voice booms over the stilled conversation.

Viking frowns and shakes his head. "You're wasting your time, Paulie."

But he's not looking at the man. He's looking at me. "I told you; I'm staying."

The man chuckles. "They all say that at first." The woman steps forward, and she holds out a brown envelope and some paperwork that I take to be the contract.

"Here's a sign-on bonus. And I'll triple the danger pay."

The room goes silent, and all eyes are on Viking. Barrels sets his fork down, and Nate stiffens next to me.

"Six months, Chris. It's the easiest money you'll even make." Viking stares at the envelope and swallows.

He takes the contract, and my body sags. I put my

elbows on the table, and my head sinks into my hands. Viking's really leaving, and my heart breaks all over again.

The sound of paper tearing has my head jerking upwards.

Viking stares straight at me as he rips the contract into pieces. "I left once, and I'm not leaving again."

Paulie's eyes go wide. "This is life-changing money. You'd be a fool not to take it."

Without breaking eye contact, he flings the scraps of paper into the air. "And I'd be a fool to leave."

The paper flutters down around him to the floor.

My stomach unclenches, and my chest fills with hope.

"He's staying," I whisper.

Paulie's assistant ducks to the ground to pick up the scattered papers. Viking steps around her, still looking at me, and there's a question in his expression.

"I'm really staying, cupcake."

And for the first time, I believe him.

I push my chair out from the table so hard it tips backwards.

Viking strides around the table, and I move toward him on shaky legs. Tears sting my eyes, and I blink them away as he meets me in the middle.

"I will not leave you again, Sydney. Ever. And if this is what I have to do to prove it to you, then I will."

He takes a small box out of his pocket as he slides down on one knee.

I gasp, and my hands cover my mouth.

"I walked away from you once, and I'll never do that again. I want you by my side always. Sydney, will you marry me?"

He opens the box to reveal a simple gold band with an emerald set in the middle. My birthstone and the same color as my eyes. It's perfect.

The last of the hurt dissolves, and my heart dares to hope. All the heartache, the lonely nights, the shattered dreams don't matter. In the ring I see a new hope, a real commitment. Safety and security with the man I love.

"Yes," I gasp. "Yes, I'll marry you."

The room erupts into whoops as I fling myself into Viking's arms. He staggers under my weight, and we almost topple to the floor before he catches me and pulls me up with him.

Tears stream from my eyes, but they're happy tears.

Our lips collide, and heat jumps through my body. Our hips bump together and it's electric, making me push my body against his, wanting more. The whoops turn to catcalls, and we break apart as I remember we're in a room full of bikers and kids.

Nate is the first to congratulate us. He pulls me into a hug and then Viking. But I hear him mutter in his ear, "You hurt her again and I'll gut you."

Viking chuckles. "No chance of that, brother. I'm here for good."

Nate nods, and his expression softens. "Come for dinner tomorrow. Get to know your nieces."

The entire club streams past us to offer their congratulations.

Paulie is the last, and he shakes Viking's hand ruefully. "I don't understand it."

"You will when you meet the right person," Viking says.

"I'm married to the job. I get to travel. I have a nice flat, secure investments." Paulie shakes his head like he can't understand why anyone would choose anything else.

I see the life Viking could have had. Job security and adventure, but instead he chose love. He chose me. I squeeze his hand a little tighter.

Viking slaps Paulie on the back.

"Try Hope for recruits. There's a SEAL team cooling their heels."

Paulie cocks his head. "Oh yeah, what happened?"

"A mission went bad. The details are classified, but I heard one man lost his life and another lost his speech."

We were all devastated to hear about the damaged ex-SEALs on the other side of the mountain. The club went to pay their respects at the funeral of the man who didn't make it home.

"Some of those men might be interested in private work," says Viking. "They've got some aches and pains and not all of them on the outside. But I bet you'll find someone who wants an adventure. Speak to Joel. Tell him Viking sent you."

"I'll do that."

"But please, stay and eat with us first."

Another place is set for Paulie and his assistant. And

by the end of the night, I reckon he's half-convinced to give it all up and stay on the mountain.

Viking tucks me into his side, and I snuggle against his warm body.

"I told you I'm home, cupcake. Forever."

And this time, I believe him.

EPILOGUE

SYDNEY

Four years later…

*B*arrels raises his glass and peers at the frothy light ale as he swirls it around his glass. A smile spreads across his face.

"To Wild Taste Pale Ale, the newest ale on the mountain."

Cheers erupt around the room, and everyone raises matching glasses. I lift mine carefully, trying not to wake the baby sleeping on my chest.

This one is just like her father. She'll sleep through anything, even a room full of bikers celebrating their newest beer.

I raise the glass to my lips and sip the cool liquid. Its bitter taste makes my taste buds spring to life, then the sweet undertones kick in to make up for the bitterness.

"Not bad," I murmur to Viking.

He has his glass in one hand and our one-year-old toddler on his hip who's trying to swipe the beer glass.

"You want to try?"

Viking lets Leo capture the glass. He pulls it towards him, and his face screws up in disgust when he sniffs the heady beer.

"Yucky. Don't like."

Viking chuckles. "I'll remind you of that when you're sixteen and stealing these out of my fridge."

The entire club has come out to celebrate the new brew. Even Lone Star and Trish are down from the mountain. Lone Star sits in the corner with one of his girls on his knee and his other hand firmly entwined with Trish's.

Specs is seated near them with a heavily pregnant Cassie, and I bet they're wondering when they can get away to read.

Maisie barrels past chased by Bettie, Danni and Colter's eldest. Leo squirms in his arms, wanting to be put down to follow the other kids.

Danni follows behind the kids, and she smile when she sees Leo. "You want to come play, little guy?"

Leo stares at Danni with her perfectly coifed hair and bright lipstick. I think he's half in love with his Auntie Danni. Everyone is an auntie or uncle here. Our kids are growing up with one large family and plenty of cousins.

Viking sets Leo down, and he snatches Danni's hand as she leads him off to the corner where the kids are. I'll go take my turn minding the kids soon, but first I want to enjoy a few moments with my man and enjoy the celebration of the new beer.

Viking slides his arms around me, and I lean against him. With my man behind me and my baby asleep on my chest, I let out a long contented sigh.

With his free hand, Viking runs it casually up and down my arm, giving me goosebumps and making me wonder how soon we can sneak out of here and get the kids to bed early.

"There are a lot of people who go into making the brewery what it is, and I couldn't have done it without the woman who keeps the place running—our operations Manager, Sydney Erikson."

All heads turn to me, and I raise my glass and catch Barrels's eye across the room. It's nice to get recognition for the work I do. But there are others that need recognizing too.

I stand up straight and make my voice carry across the room. "And I couldn't have kept the brewery running without the support of the entire club. I'd like to acknowledge the unsung heroes of the Wild Riders MC."

I spy Danni in the corner with three kids around her. "Danni, who minds the kids, allowing me to keep working..." I search the crowd for Maggie and find her wrapped in Arlo's arms. "And Maggie, who keeps the cookie supply coming." I look for my other lifeline and find him with a kid on one shoulder and his wife tucked into his other. "And Davis for the coffee that keeps the brewery running."

There's cheers all around, and glasses are raised.

I get an appreciative look from Raiden. As Club Prez, he knows how important it is to have the club working together.

Barrels goes on to thank his team of brewers, the distributors, Isla, who does marketing, and finally his wife, Charlie, who does the tasting events.

There's hope that the new pale ale will be another award winner, bringing more prosperity to the club.

I lean against Viking and sigh contentedly. The club is our family, our place of work, and our home.

Four years ago, I gave him a second chance, and I'm so glad he did.

* * *

BONUS CONTENT

Not ready to say goodbye to Viking and Sydney? Have a peek what family life looks like six years on. Read the Wild Return bonus scene when you sign up to the Sadie King newsletter.

Read the bonus scene at:
authorsadieking.com/bonus-scenes

Already a subscriber? Check your last email for the link that will take you straight to all the bonus content and free books.

WHAT TO READ NEXT

A SEAL'S HEART

Ed's a wounded warrior and Avery's his best friend's little sister. She doesn't know the terrible secret he keeps about her brother...

The blast that killed my best friend, Jake, also ended my career as a Navy SEAL.

I'm left unable to speak and lusting after my speech therapist, who also happens to be Jake's little sister.

Grief is hard on Avery, and I'm here for her, however she needs me.

If it's release she needs, that's what I'll give her, as long as she doesn't ask me to stay. It's the one thing this orphan doesn't know how to do. And Avery deserves better than a scarred veteran who can't speak.

Besides, if Avery knew the classified information from our final mission, she wouldn't want anything to do with me.

A SEAL's Heart is an emotional romance featuring a wounded hero and the curvy woman who heals his heart.

Keep reading for an excerpt...

A SEAL'S HEART

CHAPTER ONE

My jaw throbs and my stomach aches with hunger. I haven't eaten since the sloppy muck from the feeding tube that passes for food at the clinic this morning. But fucked if I'm going to draw more attention than I already have by attempting to stuff a sausage roll or mini sandwich into my wired shut mouth.

"Anyone for another drink?" Marcus raises his empty glass. "May as well make use of the free bar. It's what Jake would have wanted."

Jake would have wanted to be here, having a beer at The Landing and talking shit with his buddies.

I shake my head and grunt, which is all the sound I'm able to make.

"Eloquent as ever," Marcus quips.

I scowl at him. It cost me to grunt, and I'm not going to give him a second one. I've never been one for words, and my former teammates think it's hilarious that my mouth is wired shut.

The Landing was the perfect choice for Jake's wake. It's run by an ex-Marine, and the entire bar is an homage to the Navy. Navy blue vinyl covers the booths; thick ropes separate the dining area from the bar; and pictures of local service members decorate the walls.

I came here with Jake the two times I came back to his hometown in the mountains of North Carolina on leave with him.

"Did you ever come here when this place was JayJays?" Hudson rolls his broad shoulders and cricks his neck. His short dark hair is as wild as he ever lets it get. He's the only Navy SEAL who never took advantage of the fact that we could be as hairy as we wanted.

I shake my head.

"It was a dive," Hudson says. "Sticky floors and reeked like stale beer." A ghost of a smile appears on his face. "Jake loved it. We snuck in when we were underage. Jake used his brother's ID."

Amos frowns. "That little shit." He shakes his head and smiles, making him appear so much like his brother that I have to turn away.

"How long you home for?" Marcus asks.

"They gave me a month, but I'm heading back in a few days."

No one needs to ask him why. Amos is the only one of us in any shape to re-deploy. He wants payback for his brother's death.

I wonder what he'd think if he knew what happened in those final few moments of Jake's life.

But I can't tell him, even if I wanted to. The officer

investigating what went wrong with the mission came to interview me in the hospital. I wrote my statement as best I could with my fingers swollen like sausages from the impact injury. The guy got frustrated that I couldn't talk. He left me alone, but there will be a reckoning. The truth will come out at some point. But that's not what I'm thinking of today.

A swish of blue has my head snapping around so hard I almost tear the wiring in my jaw. In a sea of military uniforms and funeral black, Jake's little sister wore bright blue.

I watched her through the funeral. Who wouldn't? Avery stood with her back straight as the blue dress caressed her ankles. Her lips trembled as she held her mother's hand, their father tall and unmoving behind them in his Rear Admiral uniform. Her brother, Amos, stood on the other side of their mom, ready to prop her up if needed.

Avery held it together until the lowering of the coffin. Then the trembling of her lip erupted into a full-blown sob.

The ache in my jaw I can handle, but watching Jake's little sister cry her way through her brother's funeral is enough to make my chest implode.

The last time I saw Jake's little sister, she was just a girl. But there's nothing girlish about the woman making the rounds of grieving relatives, old friends, and military personal.

My gaze follows her as she carries a plate of sausage rolls to a group of elderly folk in the booth near the bar.

"How are you doing?" I tear my gaze away from Avery to find Joel staring at me.

His intense gaze misses nothing, as intense at home as he was when he was my commander on the battlefield.

I shrug, because the fucker knows I can't talk.

"I got you this." He pulls a notepad out of his pocket with a pen attached to it by a string. "So you can still talk to us."

I glare at the notepad and back at Joel. He looks expectant, probably waiting for me to write him a thank you note.

I grab the notepad and scribble off a note, then turn it towards him.

He reads it out loud. "What makes you think I want to talk to you fuckers?"

Joel chuckles. "You still got your voice, Ed. Don't retreat inside yourself."

He leans in. "Listen, I'm thinking of starting up this thing." He rubs the stubble on his beard. "I been thinking about it for a while, ever since I got out."

The Navy honorably discharged Joel two years ago when his wife got sick. He was the best commander in the field. I trusted him with my life. It's no mean feat to lead a team of hardened Navy SEALs, and Joel's the only commander that earned my respect. He loved the battle; he loved being a part of it. He'd be the first out leading his men from the front.

But he gave it all up without hesitation when his wife got cancer. He came back to Hope, to his family, and nursed her through the last months of her life.

"I've been doing some work with the Veterans Association in Charlotte."

I nod my head. Since I can't speak, I've become a good listener.

"The VA is great. But I've been tossing around ideas of other ways to help. I've been doing some work with veterans on the mountain. But I want something more permanent. There are a lot more people I could reach."

That's Joel for you, always thinking of how he can help.

"I'm still getting my plan together, but I might have some work coming in soon that I need some guys for." He leans in, and I get the full Joel stare.

But if he's thinking of me, then he's not thinking straight.

Two weeks ago, I was on a top secret mission in Columbia, a place where the US military should not have been. Now I'm at the funeral of my best friend with my jaw wired shut, unsure if I'll ever speak again. My career is over, and I've lost my best friend. My only friend.

I grunt. Joel deserves a grunt.

"You don't have to say anything yet." He chuckles at his own joke, and my scowl deepens. "Get yourself fixed up. Find your voice, then let's talk."

I may never talk again, is what the doctor told me. The shrapnel from the explosion got me on the left side of my face. My body is fine. I'm in one piece. My legs work, my arms are okay now that the swelling has gone down. But I took the hit on my jaw. My first reconstructive surgery is next week. Then they'll see if my tongue can strengthen and repair itself enough for me to talk.

Fuck that. No one needs to hear me speak. I've just lost my career, the only thing I was good at, and I've lost my best buddy. Who the fuck do I need to talk to?

My gaze catches on the swish of a skirt. I turn too late and find Avery standing before us. Joel stands up, and I'm two beats behind him.

"I'm sorry for your loss," Joel says.

I stand up too quick, and my big ugly mug catches on the end of the tray of sausage rolls. The plate clatters to the ground, and sausage rolls fall with soft thuds on the vinyl floor.

Avery covers her mouth with her hand as the entire room stops to stare at us.

Fucking great.

I duck to the floor at the same time she does, and our bodies collide. She bounces off me, and on instinct I shoot my arm out to catch her. I grip her around the waist and catch her from falling to the floor.

She stares up at me, her mouth in a perfect surprised 'O.'

She wears her hair pulled back into a bun with wispy strands framing her face. Her raw beauty enhanced by a thin layer of make-up.

Sorry.

The word forms in my mind, but all that comes out is a grunt. An animalistic grunt that matches the beast I've become.

She frowns in confusion, and her gaze shifts from my

eyes to my swollen cheek and the pieces of wire poking out between my cracked lips. I close my lips around my tin gums and my mouth slants to the side, deformed and hideous.

I can't bear to watch Avery's gaze turn to pity. I set her abruptly on the floor and turn away.

I should stick around to pick up the sausage rolls, but I can't bear to be around Avery any longer. I don't deserve to be here with her family, grieving. I don't deserve their hospitality, and I sure as hell don't deserve her pity.

Not when I'm the one responsible for her brother's death.

* * *

Wild Heart Mountain

Jake's Heroes

These ex-Navy SEALs will do anything for the women they fall for. Expect wounded warriors in these emotional and steamy stories of love and healing.

Military Heroes

Kobe brings together a group of military veterans who live on the side of Wild Heart Mountain. Can these wounded warriors find love or do their scars cut too deep?

Wild Riders MC

This group of ex-military bikers fall hard and fall fast when they encounter the curvy women who heal their hearts.

Mountain Heroes

Steamy stories featuring the men and women from Wild Heart Mountain's Search and Rescue and Fire service.

Biker Brothers of Winter Town

Short, sweet tales of men who ride and the curvy women who claim their hearts.

A Runaway Bride for Christmas

A snowstorm keeps this runaway bride trapped in the cabin of the mountain's biggest grump.

Sunset Coast

Underground Crows MC

Short and steamy MC romance stories of obsessed men and curvy girls.

Sunset Security

A security firm run by ex-military men who become obsessed with their curvy girls.

Men of the Sea

Super short and steamy tales from Temptation Bay of bad boys and curvy girls.

Love and Obsession

A bad boy trilogy featuring a thief, a henchman and an ex-military hitman who finds redemption with his curvy girl.

Filthy Rich Love

The billionaires of the Sunset Coast. These alpha men fall hard and fall fast for the younger curvy women who crash into their world.

Maple Springs

Small Town Sisters

Five curvy sister's inherit a dog hotel. But can they find love? Short and steamy instalove romance!

Candy's Café

A small-town cafe that's all heart. Meet the sister's who run it and the customer's who keep coming back.

All the Single Dads

These single dad hotties are fiercely protective and will do anything for the ones they love.

Men of Maple Mountain

These men are OTT possessive and will stop at nothing to claim the curvy innocent women they become obsessed with.

The Carter Family

Blue collar men find love with curvy girls in these quick read instalove romances.

Curvy Girls Can

Short, sweet and steamy instalove stories about sassy curvy women and the men who love them.

The Biker Brother's Curvy Christmas

Hot Santas, curvy girls and bikers. A feel good Christmas romance duet.

The Seal's Obsession

A soft stalker, secret baby, military romance. Featuring an OTT obsessed alpha male and a sassy curvy girl.

For a full list of Sadie King's books check out her website

www.authorsadieking.com

ABOUT THE AUTHOR

Sadie King is a USA Today Best Selling Author of contemporary romance novellas.

She lives in New Zealand with her ex-military husband and raucous young son.

When she's not writing she loves catching waves with her son, running along the beach, and drinking good wine with a book in hand.

Keep in touch when you sign up for her newsletter. You'll snag yourself a free short romance and access to all the bonus content!

authorsadieking.com/bonus-scenes